Craven – Pamlico – Carteret
Regional Library

The WILD Thornberrys

The Best Valentine

by Adam Beechen

illustrated by Patrick J. Dene, Bradley J. Gake, and Mike Giles

Simon Spotlight/Nickelodeon

New York   London   Toronto   Sydney   Singapore

Discovery Facts

Beavers are a type of large rodent. Because they spend much of their lives in the water, they have two different kinds of hair: long, tough hair on top, and a softer layer of hair underneath that keeps the beaver warm in cold water. A beaver usually pairs with the same mate for its whole life. Their babies are called **kits**. Kits can swim when they're only a few hours old.

KLaSKY CSUPO Inc.

SIMON SPOTLIGHT
An imprint of Simon & Schuster Children's Publishing Division
1230 Avenue of the Americas, New York, New York 10020

Based on the TV series *The Wild Thornberrys*® created by Klasky Csupo, Inc. as seen on Nickelodeon®

Copyright © 2001 Viacom International Inc. All rights reserved. NICKELODEON, *The Wild Thornberrys*, and all related titles, logos, and characters are trademarks of Viacom International Inc. All rights reserved including the right of reproduction in whole or in part in any form. SIMON SPOTLIGHT and colophon are registered trademarks of Simon & Schuster. Manufactured in the United States of America.
First Edition   ISBN 0-689-83796-8

2 4 6 8 10 9 7 5 3 1

Eliza Thornberry stepped out of the Commvee and her feet sank into the mud.

"Gosh!" she exclaimed to Darwin, looking at all the downed trees and overturned rocks and bushes. "The river must have flooded!"

Darwin leaped to the branches of a tree and picked mud from his toes. "I'll just stay up here," he said.

"Darwin, come down! Today is Valentine's Day, and I need your help!" Eliza said. "Every year I make Mom and Dad a present out of things I find. I know we can find something really special for them here in Alaska."

Just then, Debbie looked out of the Commvee.

"Gross!" she said when she saw the mud. She looked down at Eliza. "Don't tell me you're going out in the mud to look for your dopey present for Mom and Dad."

"It's not dopey, it's cool!" Eliza replied. "Want to help?"

Are you kidding?" Debbie answered. "I ordered a present for Mom and Dad on the Internet. And besides, mud does *not* go with my outfit."

"Marianne and Nigel stepped outside, holding hands.

"Nigel, let's see if we can film some moose courting!" Marianne said excitedly.

"Love is in the air," Nigel agreed, grabbing their camera equipment.

As they were leaving camp, Nigel called to Eliza, "We'll be back early, poppet! I want everyone to be here to see my Valentine's Day present to your mother! It's quite romantic!"

Eliza put her small video camera into her backpack and smiled at Donnie and Darwin. "Let's go!" she cried.

Eliza and Donnie walked along the river, looking for things for her present, while Darwin leaped from branch to branch in the trees above.

"Darwin, come down here and help!" Eliza yelled.

"Why?" Darwin replied. "It's not muddy up here!"

Eliza was about to answer when a worried-looking beaver ran past.

"Oh, no! Oh, no!" he cried.

"What's the matter?" Eliza asked.

"The flood washed me away from my dam," the beaver explained. "And now I can't find my mate. I have to get home because my family is coming! Can you help me?"

"Of course we'll help you!" Eliza said.

Darwin muttered, "What do you mean, *we?*"

"Come on, Dar," Eliza said. "He has family coming to visit! He wants to be with his mate on Valentine's Day!"

"Oh, all right," he agreed. He swung after Eliza and Donnie as they followed the beaver.

Suddenly, Eliza heard a rustling in the nearby bushes. "Mmm," someone growled in a nasty voice. "I smell lunch!" Eliza and her friends turned to see three hungry-looking wolves.

The beaver dove into the river. "No time for lunch!" he cried to the wolves. "I've got to get home to my family!"

Darwin was shaking, he was so scared of the wolves. "What should we do, Eliza?" he cried.

"We'll go where the beaver went," Eliza told him. "The wolves won't follow us into the water!"

Eliza leaped off the riverbank onto a log that was moving quickly in the water. Darwin jumped off his branch and landed next to her. The wolves growled in anger as the water carried Eliza, her friends, and the beaver away.

Back at the Commvee, Debbie heard a thump outside. Racing outside, she saw the package the mail plane had dropped for them.

"It's finally here! The Documentarian's Transcription Assistor I ordered! With an important name like that, Mom and Dad are sure to love it," she said to herself.

Back on shore, Eliza, Darwin, Donnie, and the beaver rounded a bend in the river. Suddenly, the beaver cried, "There it is! That's my dam!" Just then, four large brown bears came crashing out of the trees and into the water, where they started to fish.

"Uh-oh. Bears get very angry if you bother them when they're fishing," Eliza said. "We'll have to wait until they're done."

"I can't wait!" the beaver insisted. "My family is coming! I have to be with them!" And he jumped into the water. Eliza knew the bears would see him. She had to act fast!

Eliza hurried back upstream around the bend of the river. She could see the beaver swimming toward the bears, but they hadn't noticed him yet.

"Wow," she said loudly so the bears could hear her, "there are so many fish over here! This is a great place to fish!"

The bears looked up. "Fish? Over there?" the largest bear said eagerly. The bears started making their way toward the sound of Eliza's voice as the beaver swam safely into his dam. Eliza sighed in relief and hurried back to her friends.

Eliza, Donnie, and Darwin jumped from stone to stone in the river until they got to the dam. Eliza heard squeaking sounds and bent down to look inside. There she saw the beaver, his mate, and a litter of tiny newborn beaver kits!

"So this is what you meant when you said your family was coming!" she exclaimed. "You were about to be a father!"

Eliza took her video camera out of her backpack. "If it's all right, I'd like to film you. It will make the perfect Valentine's present for my mom and dad!"

Back at camp, Eliza showed her parents the video she had made of the beavers.

"It's smashing, Eliza!" Nigel said.

Marianne ruffled Eliza's hair. "It's a lovely present, honey," she said.

"Happy Valentine's Day, Mom and Dad. I love you," Eliza said. She hugged her parents tightly.

"I got you something too!" Debbie exclaimed, holding out her box.

Nigel tore open the present. "It's a Documentarian's Transcription Assistor!" he said.

Debbie stared. "It's a pencil? Man, what a rip-off! I didn't know exactly what I got you, but I was sure it was something *special!*"

Marianne smiled. "Debbie, it's perfect! Our pencil broke today while we were filming." She and Nigel kissed Debbie. "It's a very thoughtful gift."

"It is?" Debbie asked. "I mean, yeah, sure it is! Happy Valentine's Day!"

"And now," Nigel said grandly, "It's time for my present to you, Marianne! Something romantic to say 'I love you.'"

"Oh, honey," Marianne started to protest. "That's sweet, but we need to start editing! We don't have time!"

"Marianne, there's always time for romance," Nigel said, with a twinkle in his eye. He rushed to the Commvee and returned a moment later with his guitar. He cleared his throat, then sang,

"I'm your loving husband, and you're my dearest wife!
Like a family of beavers, we're together for life! . . ."

Eliza smiled, thinking about the beaver and his family. It didn't matter if you lived in a Commvee or a dam, she thought, the best Valentine's Day gift is to be with the ones you love!